Stark
www.
330.4

FEB -

D1084082

DISCARDED

Carlos & Carmen

The Pet Show Problem

by Kirsten McDonald
illustrated by Erika Meza

Calico Kid

An Imprint of Magic Wagon
abdopublishing.com

For Nana'E who would have clapped the
loudest and longest at the pet show —KKM

For Elliott, who arrived on book 1 and left on book 9,
and for Pusskin, who took over in the end. —EM

abdopublishing.com

Published by Magic Wagon, a division of ABDO, PO Box 398166, Minneapolis, Minnesota 55439. Copyright © 2017 by Abdo Consulting Group, Inc. International copyrights reserved in all countries. No part of this book may be reproduced in any form without written permission from the publisher. Calico Kid™ is a trademark and logo of Magic Wagon.

Printed in the United States of America, North Mankato, Minnesota.
102016
012017

THIS BOOK CONTAINS
RECYCLED MATERIALS

Written by Kirsten McDonald
Illustrated by Erika Meza
Edited by Heidi M.D. Elston
Design Contributors: Christina Doffing & Candice Keimig

Publisher's Cataloging in Publication Data

Names: McDonald, Kirsten, author. | Meza, Erika, illustrator.
Title: The pet show problem / by Kirsten McDonald ; illustrated by Erika Meza.
Description: Minneapolis, MN : Magic Wagon, 2017. | Series: Carlos & Carmen
Summary: Carlos and Carmen want their cat, Spooky, to be in a pet show. They try to teach Spooky tricks, but she's not interested. They try to make her the most beautiful cat around, but Spooky has other plans. Just when the twins are about to give up, they come up with the perfect solution to the pet show problem.
Identifiers: LCCN 2016947640 | ISBN 9781624021848 (lib. bdg.) | ISBN 9781624022449 (ebook) | ISBN 9781624022746 (Read-to-me ebook)
Subjects: LCSH: Hispanic American families--Juvenile fiction. | Twins--Juvenile fiction. | Brothers and sisters--Juvenile fiction. | Pets--Juvenile fiction.
Classification: DDC [E]--dc23
LC record available at http://lccn.loc.gov/2016947640

Table of Contents

Chapter 1
Spooky's Tricks

"¡Mira!" said Papá, showing the twins a flyer. "There's going to be a pet show."

Carlos read, "All pets welcome."

Carmen read, "Lots of prizes."

"Our cat Spooky is a good mascota," said Carlos.

"She could win a premio," said Carmen.

"Especially if we taught her some tricks," said Carlos.

Carlos looked at Carmen. Carmen looked at Carlos. "Are you thinking what I'm thinking?" they said. And because they were twins, they were.

Carlos and Carmen ran to find Spooky.

They looked on Carmen's bed. They looked on Carlos's bed.

They looked in all of Spooky's favorite spots. Finally they found her sitting on the back deck, cleaning her paws.

"Sit, Spooky," said Carlos. Spooky kept sitting. She kept cleaning her paws.

"Shake, Spooky," said Carmen. She reached out and shook Spooky's freshly cleaned paw.

"We're good at mascota training," said Carlos.

"Yes," said Carmen. "We've already taught Spooky two trucos."

Spooky stood up. She stretched out her front legs. She swished her tail.

"Fetch," said Carmen, rolling a bouncy ball.

Spooky ran. She pounced on the ball. She batted the ball around the deck.

"Bring me the ball," said Carmen. Spooky batted the ball some more.

"Sit," said Carlos. Spooky flicked the ball into the air.

"Shake," said Carmen, reaching for Spooky's paw. Spooky swished her tail and jumped out into the yard.

"I'm not sure Spooky has learned any trucos after all," said Carlos.

"Yo tampoco," agreed Carmen.

Chapter 2
Brushes and Ribbons

That afternoon, Carlos said,
"Spooky isn't good at trucos."
"No, she isn't," agreed Carmen.
"But she is a pretty gatita."

"Maybe she can win a premio for being the prettiest," said Carlos.

Carlos ran and got a brush.

Carmen ran and got some ribbons.

Then they ran into the backyard with their supplies.

"Spooky!" the twins called as they ran. "Where are you?"

They found Spooky sitting under the big tree.

Carlos brushed Spooky's back. "I'm making your fur all shiny," he told her.

Carmen tied one ribbon around Spooky's neck. She tied another around her tail. "I'm making you extra beautiful," Carmen said.

Spooky looked at the ribbon on her tail. It fluttered and flittered.

She twitched her tail. The ribbon dangled and danced.

Spooky swatted the ribbon. Then she chased the ribbon and her tail around and around.

"No, Spooky, no!" shouted Carlos and Carmen.

But Spooky didn't listen. She flopped onto the ground. She rolled back and forth.

When Spooky stood up, her fur was a mess. And, the ribbons lay in tangles under her paws.

Carlos and Carmen looked at the mess.

Carlos said, "I don't think Spooky likes this pet show plan."

"Yo tampoco," agreed Carmen.

Chapter 3
A New Plan

Carlos and Carmen sat on the back deck. Mamá and Abuelita came out and sat beside them.

"What's the matter?" Mamá asked.

"We want to be in the pet show," said Carmen.

"But Spooky won't wear a ribbon," Carlos said.

"And she won't learn any trucos," said Carmen.

"Those are problems," said Abuelita.

"We need a different mascota," said Carlos.

"Or a different kind of show," said Carmen.

All of a sudden, Carmen looked at Carlos. Carlos looked at Carmen. They both smiled big smiles.

"Are you thinking what I'm thinking?" they both said. And because they were twins, they were.

First, they got paper and markers.
Next, they made posters and tickets.
Then they got Carmen's Halloween
costume and an old bedsheet. For
the rest of the day, they planned and
practiced.

Spooky just watched. This plan did not look tasty, but it might be fun.

Chapter 4
The Pet Show

The next day, there were pet show posters all over the house. There were four pet show tickets on the breakfast table.

"What's this for?" asked Abuelita, holding up a ticket.

"It's your ticket to the show," said Carmen.

"What show?" asked Mamá.

"A special mascota show here at our house," said Carlos.

"The posters tell you all about it," said Carmen.

"Except Tío Alex can't see the posters," said Carlos. "So we need to call him."

"Sounds like fun," said Pápa.

Carlos and Carmen set up chairs in the backyard. They hung a bedsheet from the big tree.

The twins shouted, "¡Ya es hora!"

Mamá, Papá, Abuelita, and Tío Alex all came into the backyard.

27

Carlos and Carmen took their
tickets. They showed them where to
sit. Then the twins went behind the
bedsheet curtain.

Carlos came back out first. He said,
"Announcing, the Great Gatita!"

Carmen came out. She had on her
Halloween cat ears and tail.

"Sit," commanded Carlos. The Great
Gatita sat.

The audience clapped. Spooky
looked at the long, fluffy tail.

"Shake," said Carlos. The Great
Gatita shook.

The audience clapped again.
Spooky crept under Abuelita's chair.

"Fetch," said Carlos, throwing the
ball. The Great Gatita ran and got
the ball.

The audience clapped. Spooky crept under Tío Alex's chair.

"Roll," said Carlos. The Great Gatita did a somersault.

Suddenly, Spooky pounced. She grabbed the somersaulting tail with her front paws. She kicked it with

her back paws. She twisted the tail around and around.

The audience clapped and laughed.

"I guess Spooky wanted to be in the show after all," said Mamá.

Murr-uhhh, said Spooky as she ran behind the curtain.

Then everybody clapped and laughed once more. They all agreed it was the best pet show ever.

Spanish
to
English

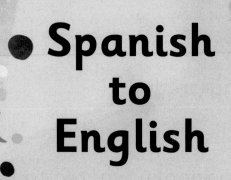

Abuelita – Grandma

gatita – girl kitten

Mamá – Mommy

mascota – pet

¡Mira! – Look!

Papá – Daddy

premio – prize

Tío – Uncle

trucos – tricks

¡Ya es hora! – It's time!

yo tampoco – me neither

3 1333 04633 0773